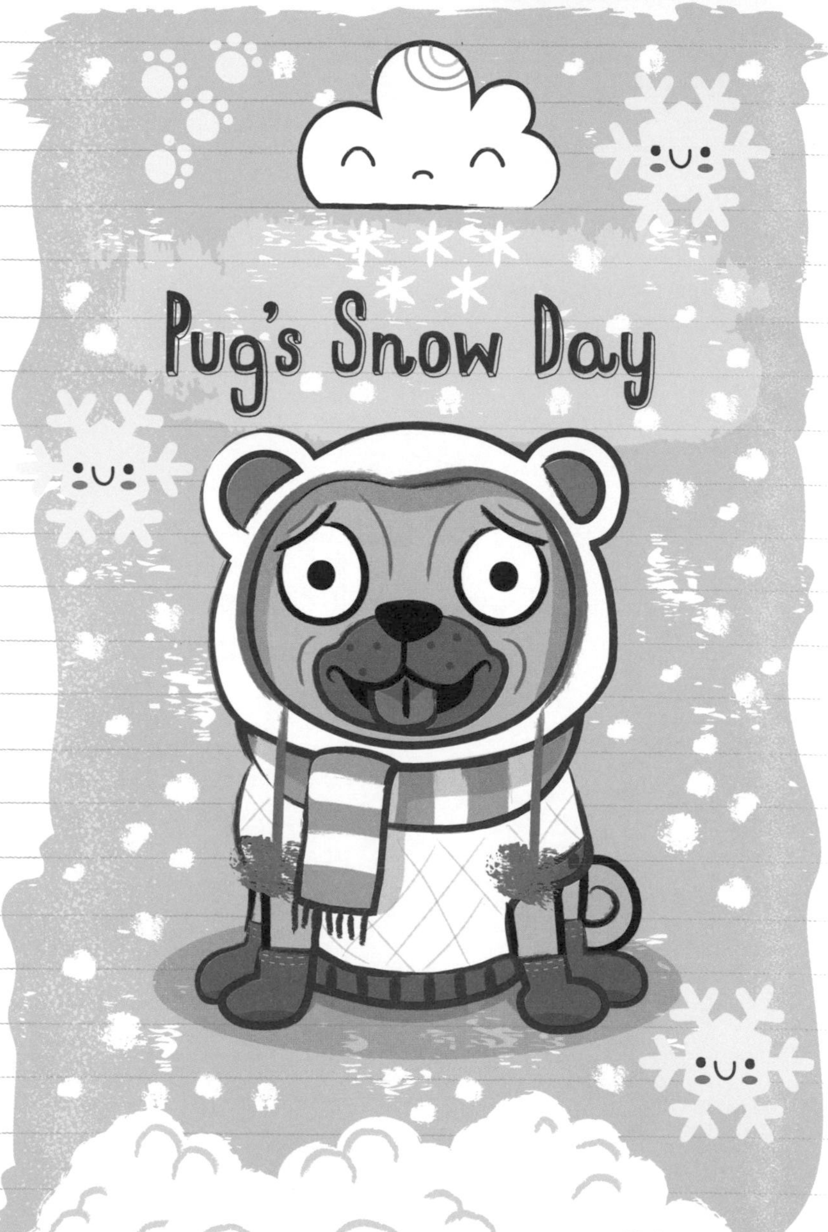
Pug's Snow Day

Read more Diary of a Pug books!

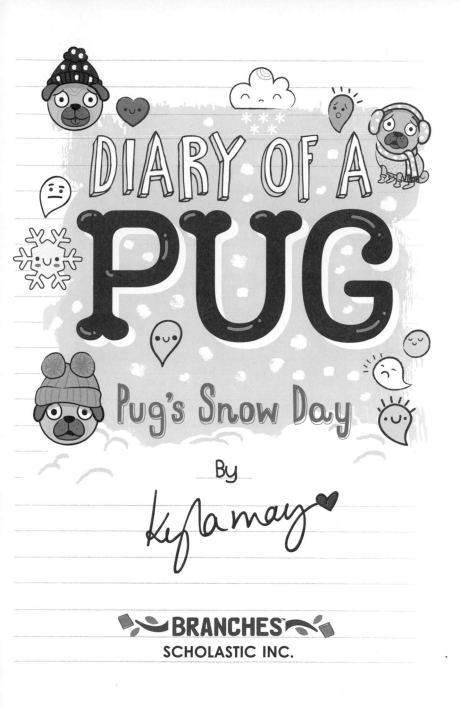

DIARY OF A PUG

Pug's Snow Day

By

Kyla May

BRANCHES

SCHOLASTIC INC.

To my amazing twins, Jaida & Kiara

Special thanks to Sonia Sander

Art copyright © 2020 by Kyla May Dinsmore
Text copyright © 2020 by Scholastic Inc.

Photos © KylaMay2019

Library of Congress Cataloging-in-Publication Data

Names: May, Kyla, author, illustrator. Title: Pug's snow day / by Kyla May. Description: First edition. I New York, NY : Branches/Scholastic Inc., 2020. I Series: Diary of a pug ; 2 I Summary: Bub the pug has never seen snow before, and when Duchess the cat tells him it is frozen rain he is appalled and does not want to go out even to play with his human, Bella—but the week is about to get worse, because a new family has moved in next door, and they apparently have a pet monster (at least if Nutz the squirrel can be believed) and Bella's mother has arranged a play date for Sunday.
Identifiers: LCCN 2019004383I ISBN 9781338530063 (digest pbk.) I ISBN 9781338530070 (reinforced library binding)
Subjects: LCSH: Pug—Juvenile fiction. I Dogs—Juvenile fiction. I Snow—Juvenile fiction. I Neighbors—Juvenile fiction. I Squirrels—Juvenile fiction. I Diaries—Juvenile fiction. I Humorous stories. I CYAC: Pug—Fiction. I Dogs—Fiction. I Snow—Fiction. I Neighbors—Fiction. I Squirrels—Fiction. I Diaries—Fiction. I Humorous stories. I LCGFT: Humorous fiction. I Diary fiction. Classification: LCC PZ7.M4535 Px 2020 I DDC 813.6 [E] —dc23 LC record available at https://lccn.loc.gov/2019004383

10 9 8 7   21 22 23 24

Printed in China   62
First edition, January 2020
Book design by Kyla May and Sarah Dvojack

Table of Contents

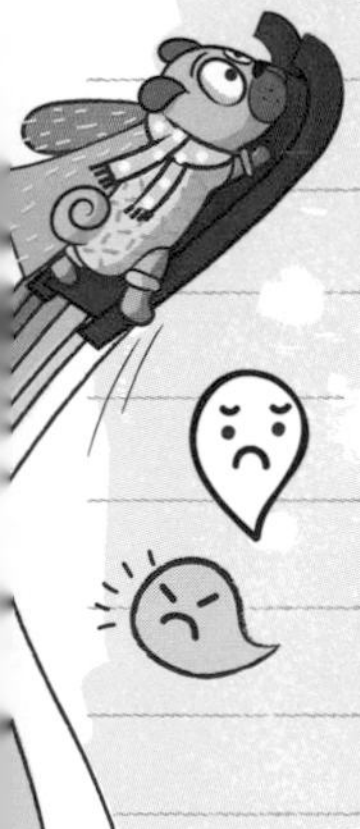

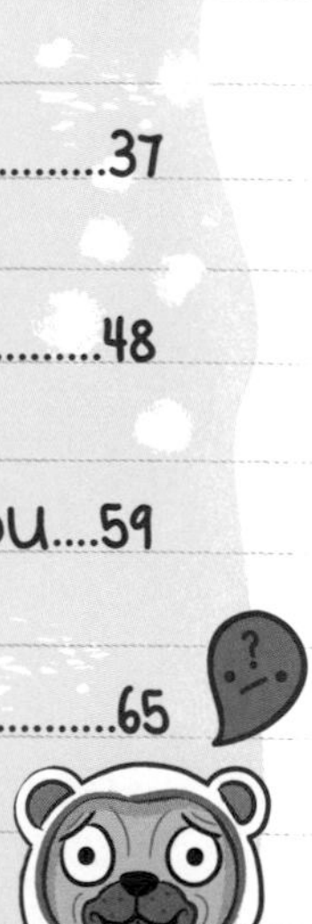

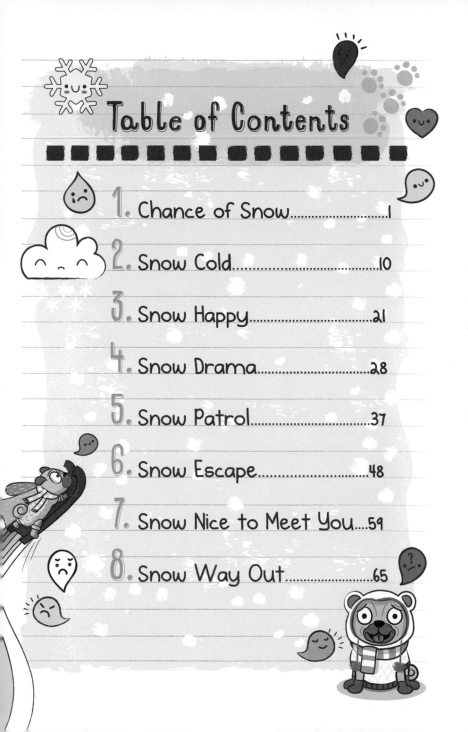

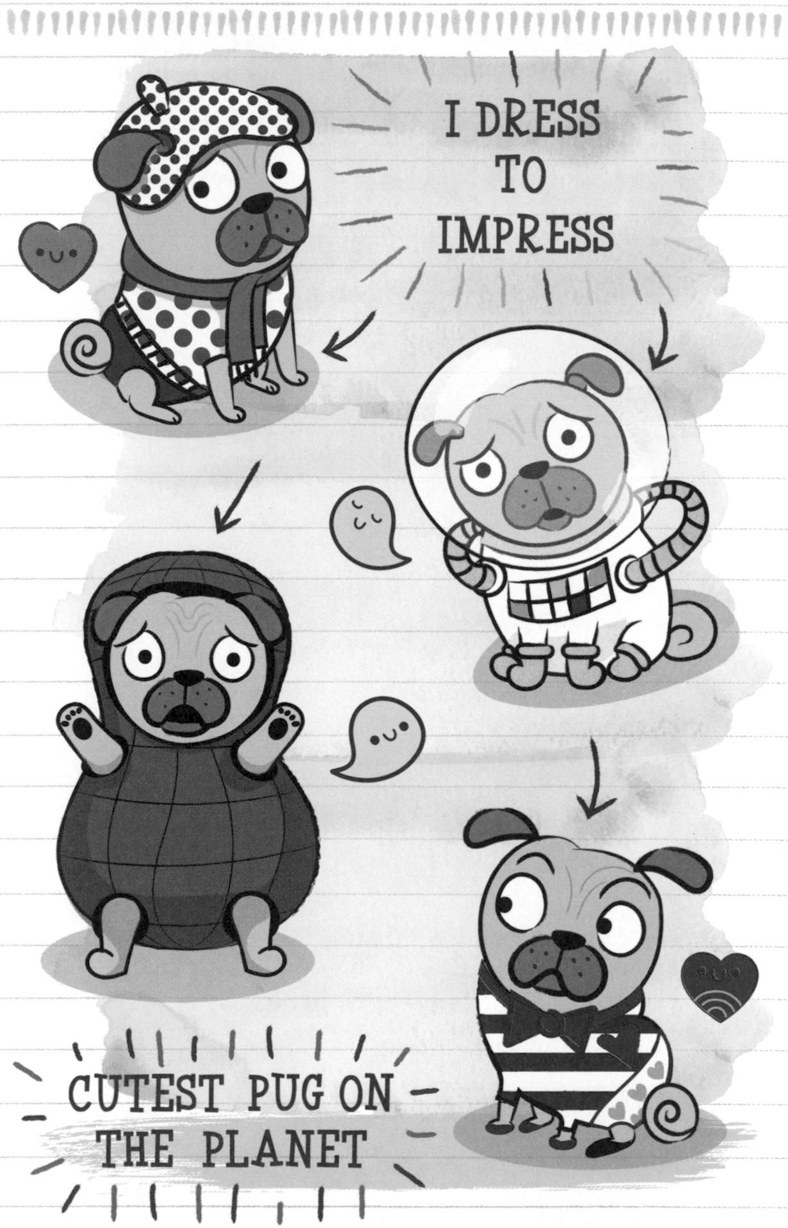
I DRESS TO IMPRESS
CUTEST PUG ON THE PLANET

Chapter 1

CHANCE OF SNOW

SUNDAY

Dear Diary,

BARON VON BUBBLES here. But everyone calls me BUB.

It's been awhile since my last entry. I've been pretty busy. Here are some things to know about me:

I always dress to impress. (Some people say I'm the cutest pug on the planet.)

I make many different faces:

Happy to See Bella Face

REALLY Have to Go Out Face

Worried Face

Nervous Face (also known as the I Just Farted Face)

Face for Duchess (Sometimes it's just easier to let her have her way.)

Duchess, you know that's my favorite chair.

Not anymore, Bubby-kins.

DUCHESS

Can you believe she calls me that? It's because she knows it annoys me.

Face for Nutz (He's always trying to get the best deal.)

I can help you if you give me the jar.

You can have one spoonful, Nutz.

NUTZ

Here are some of my favorite things:

BEAR

PEANUT BUTTER

WEEKENDS WITH BELLA

You know what is NOT my favorite?

GETTING WET!
When my human,
Bella, first brought
me home, I
jumped into
a bubble bath
with her. But eeeek!
There was WATER
under the bubbles! Bella laughed so hard.
(That's how I got my name, by the way.)

I used to avoid the rain, too. Even when
I HAD to go out to do my business. But
Bella fixed that. She built me a rain shelter
and gave me a raincoat and umbrella.

But there's one
more thing I dislike.
Can you guess what
it is? Wet kisses!
YUCK!

There's only one person I don't mind kisses from. That's Bella. She means the world to me. She adopted me when I was a pup. It was love at first sniff.

I just love you!

What is that yummy smell?

Sundays are my fun days! Bella and I play in the yard all day. Bella never gets tired of throwing sticks.

Today while we were playing, the air got cold. Then Bella pointed at the sky.

Diary, I'm not sure how I feel about snow. Bella loves it. But she also loves baths. And you know how I feel about water.

FIRST STAR

Please let there be a snow day tomorrow.

I love Bella, so I guess I wish for snow, too.

Chapter 2

SNOW COLD

MONDAY

Dear Diary,

You won't believe it. This morning, Bella woke ME up! That never, ever happens! She was so happy and loud for so early in the day.

My wish came true: It's a snow day! No school!

What time is it?

Of course, I was over the moon that I got an extra day with Bella.

Duchess gave me a look like she knew something I didn't.

But, Diary, you know how much better I am with water now. Plus, snowflakes look tiny. How bad can they be?

But I got a little nervous as we headed out the door. Bella gave me baby booties to wear! Can you imagine?

Those booties will keep your paws toasty warm, Bub.

I hope none of my friends see me in these.

I was right to be worried. But not about the booties. Snow is the worst.

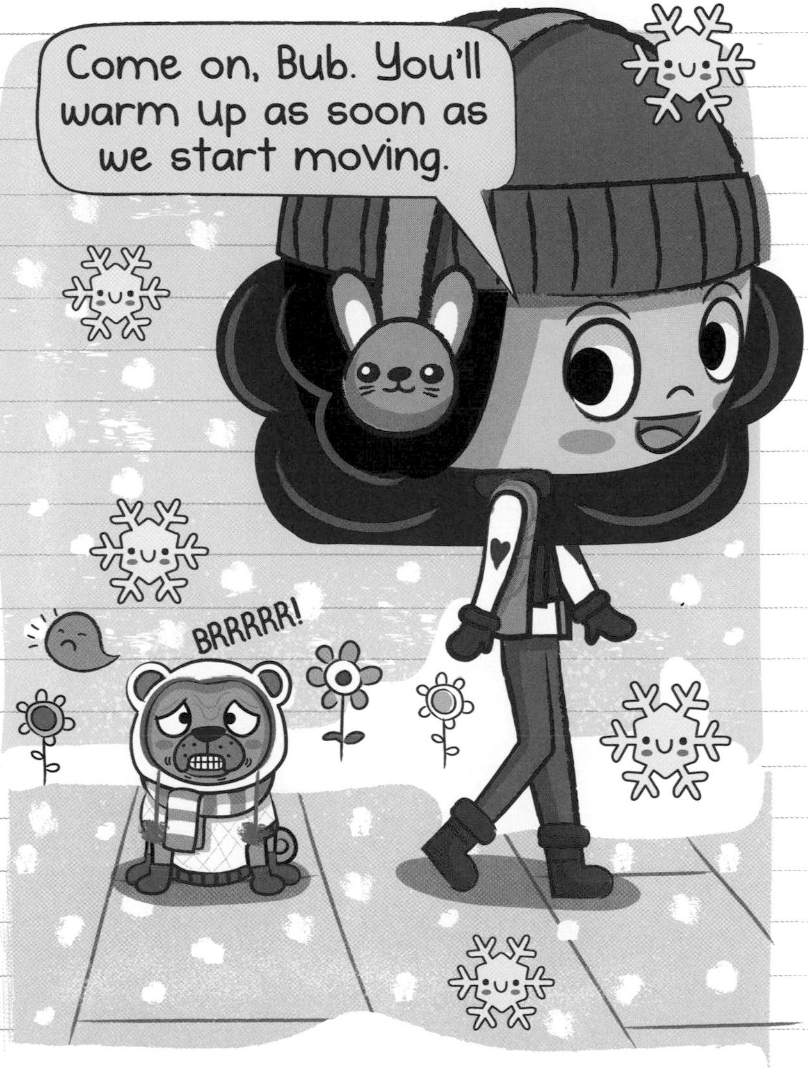
Come on, Bub. You'll warm up as soon as we start moving.
BRRRRR!

Diary, I wasn't just cold.

I slipped.

I crashed.

I sank.

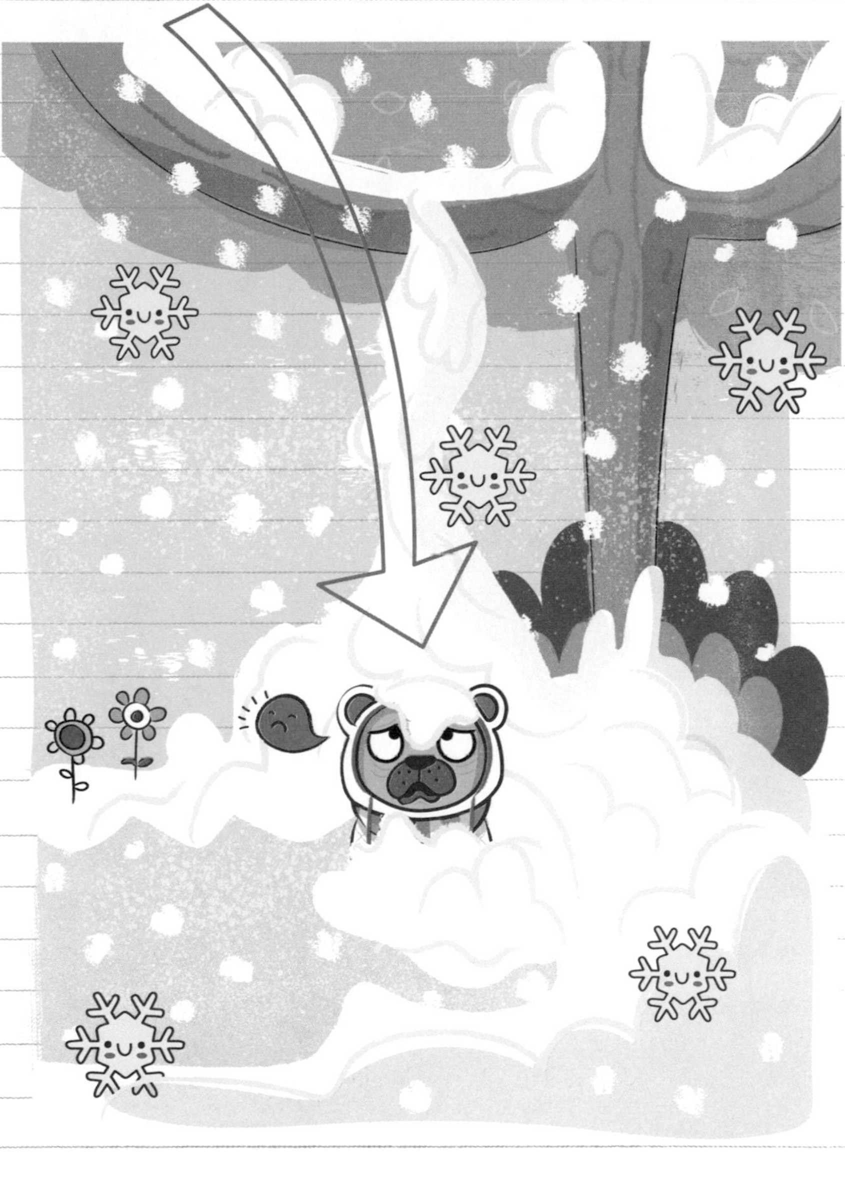

The final straw came while I was sniffing the icy ground. My nose froze to the ice! I was stuck!

Bella had to rescue me.

Luckily, Bella stopped our walk after that. She wrapped me up and carried me home.

My poor Bubby.

I hope today was my first and last snow day.

I was so happy to be going home that I didn't notice the moving truck parked outside our house. But Bella did.

Look, Bub!

We're not moving, are we?!

Then I really panicked.

This day was getting worse by the minute!

Chapter 3

SNOW HAPPY

TUESDAY

Dear Diary,

I had the worst nightmare last night. We were moving into a house made of snow!

There, there, Bubby. Are you having a bad dream?

MM-MM-MM

But it's okay now. We're not moving. I overheard Bella's mom say the truck belonged to the new neighbors.

Did I mention there was another snow day today?! All Bella wanted to do was go outside. She begged me to go with her. But my bed was so warm. And I knew how cold it was out there.

Please, Bubby! Let's go play!

Oh no! Not again!

Diary, I finally gave in. You know how much I hate disappointing Bella. But this time I made sure I was ready for the snow.

I'm all set!

Nice look! I'll be here sitting by the fire.

The snow wasn't bad now that I was properly dressed. The trick was not having to touch it. My outfit solved that problem. We made . . .

Snow pug angels

and snowpugs.

Then we built a snow fort

and had a snowball fight.

Best of all, we went sledding. It felt like skateboarding super fast downhill.
I LOVED it!

But then we heard a really loud noise from the yard next door. The ground shook. Smoke and sparks flew into the air.

Chapter 4

SNOW DRAMA

WEDNESDAY

Dear Diary,

You are not going to believe this! It snowed all night again! But at least this morning, Bella was happy to play inside. Her mom had other ideas.

Bella, go outside and play!

But there's a monster next door, Mom! I heard it! And I saw smoke and sparks!

Bella's mom told her again and again that there was no monster next door. She said it was probably the boy who just moved in. But we didn't believe her.

Bubby, I have bad news. We have a playdate with the new boy and his pet dog on Sunday.

Noooo!

Bella and I took matters into our own paws. Before Sunday, we had to find out who—or what—was living next door!

What if we don't like the new boy?

I'm more worried about his pet! That noise we heard didn't sound like a dog —it sounded like a monster!

SPY STUFF

We waited until it was quiet and the coast was clear. Then we went outside to set up our spy headquarters.

We couldn't imagine what horrible animal would make all that noise.

What kind of pet sounds like that?

A polar bear?

A lion?

Duchess?

Diary, I bet you thought yesterday sounded scary. But today was even worse. We heard loud growling and saw more smoke and sparks. The walls of our snow fort started to shake!

I think it's going to cave in!

Run, Bub!

Then the monster started throwing stuff over the fence at us. Chewed-up wood hit the ground all around us.

When we got back inside, Bella and I made a deal. We shook on it.

That's it! I am NOT going outside again!

Me neither! Well, except to do my business...

Diary, I've never seen Bella so scared. She locked herself in her room for the rest of the day. Her mom had to take me out for my afternoon walk. And Bella never misses a walk!

This won't work. I have to solve this monster mystery once and for all.

Chapter 5

SNOW PATROL

THURSDAY

Dear Diary,

Hooray! The snow finally stopped!

> I have to go to school today. Be brave, Bub!

> Don't worry about me, Bella.

It was time to set my detective plan in motion!

First I found the perfect outfit for the job.

Then I headed out to the snow fort. It wasn't long before Nutz came snooping around.

Nutz can be so nosy.

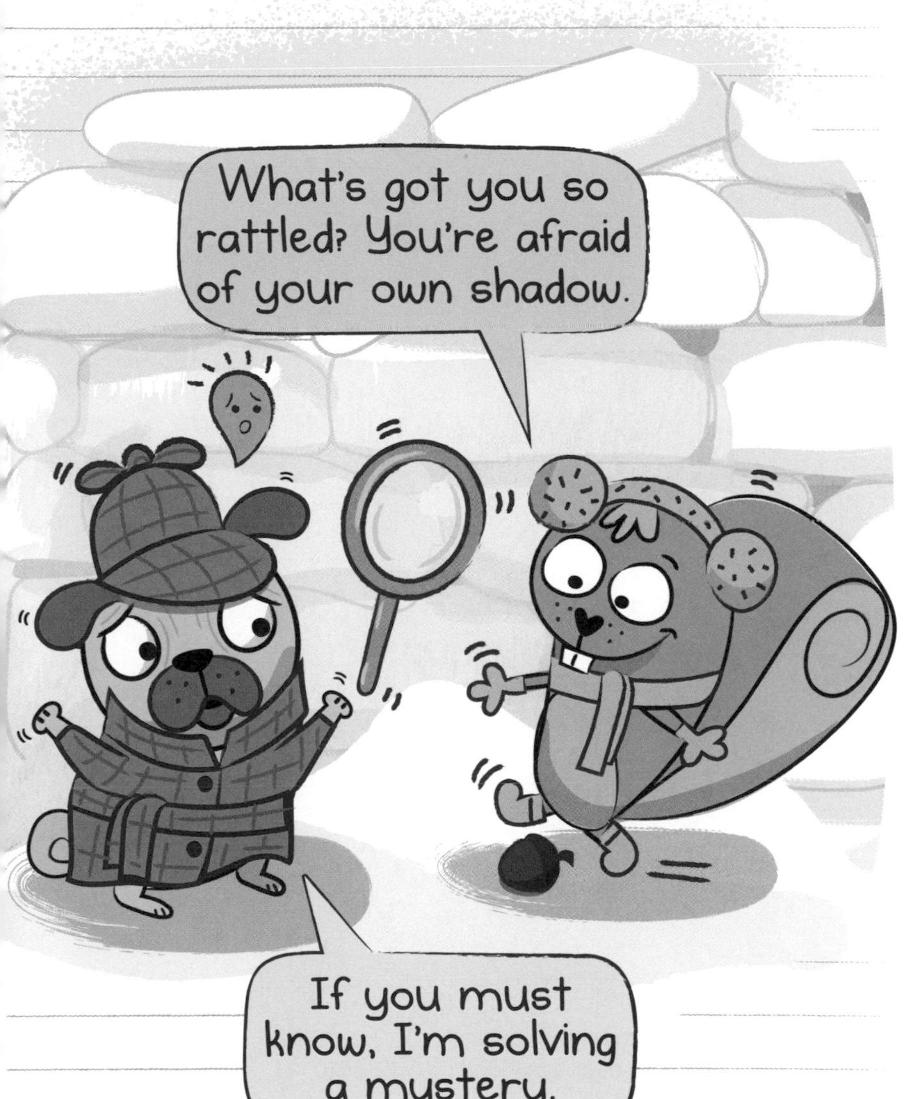
What's got you so rattled? You're afraid of your own shadow.
If you must know, I'm solving a mystery.

Diary, we both know you can't always trust Nutz. But I was a little curious about what he had to say about the monster.

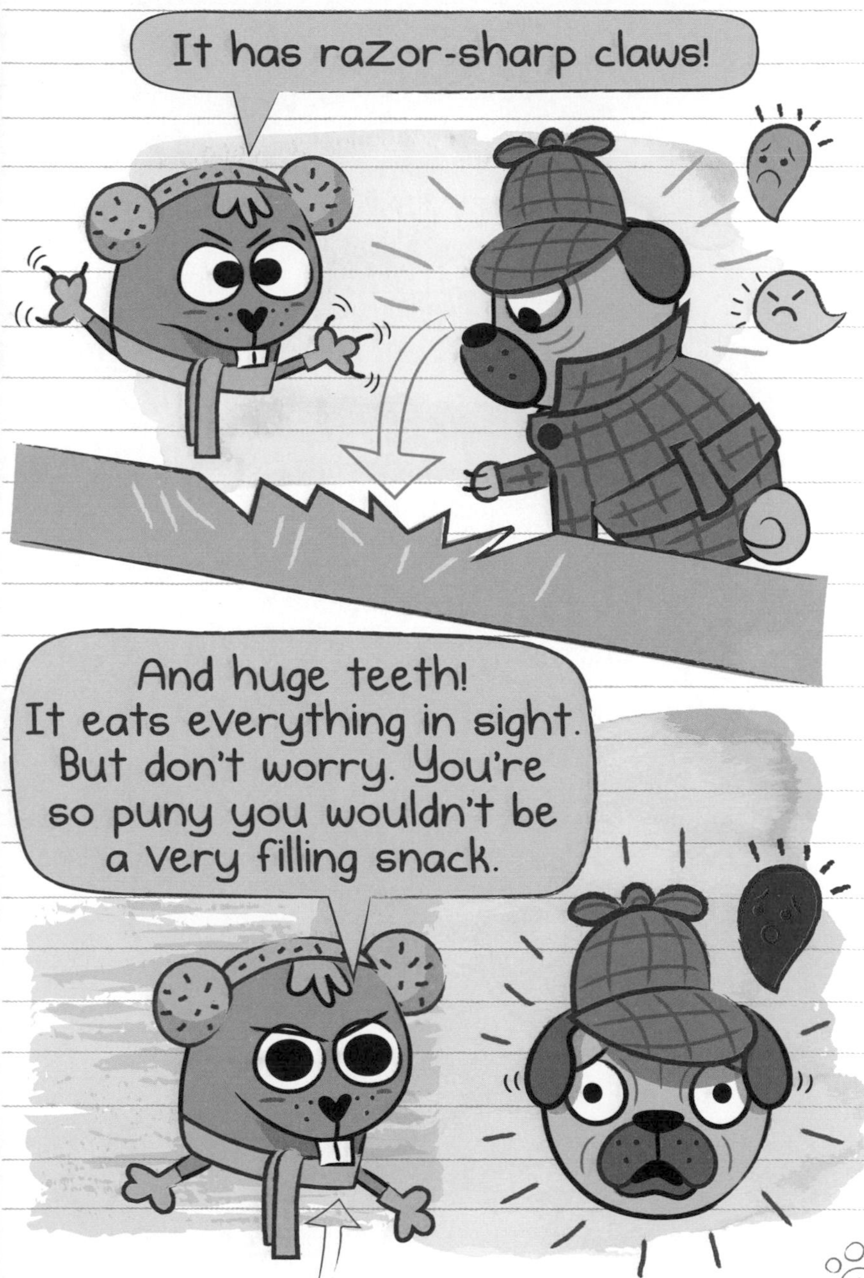
It has razor-sharp claws!
And huge teeth! It eats everything in sight. But don't worry. You're so puny you wouldn't be a very filling snack.

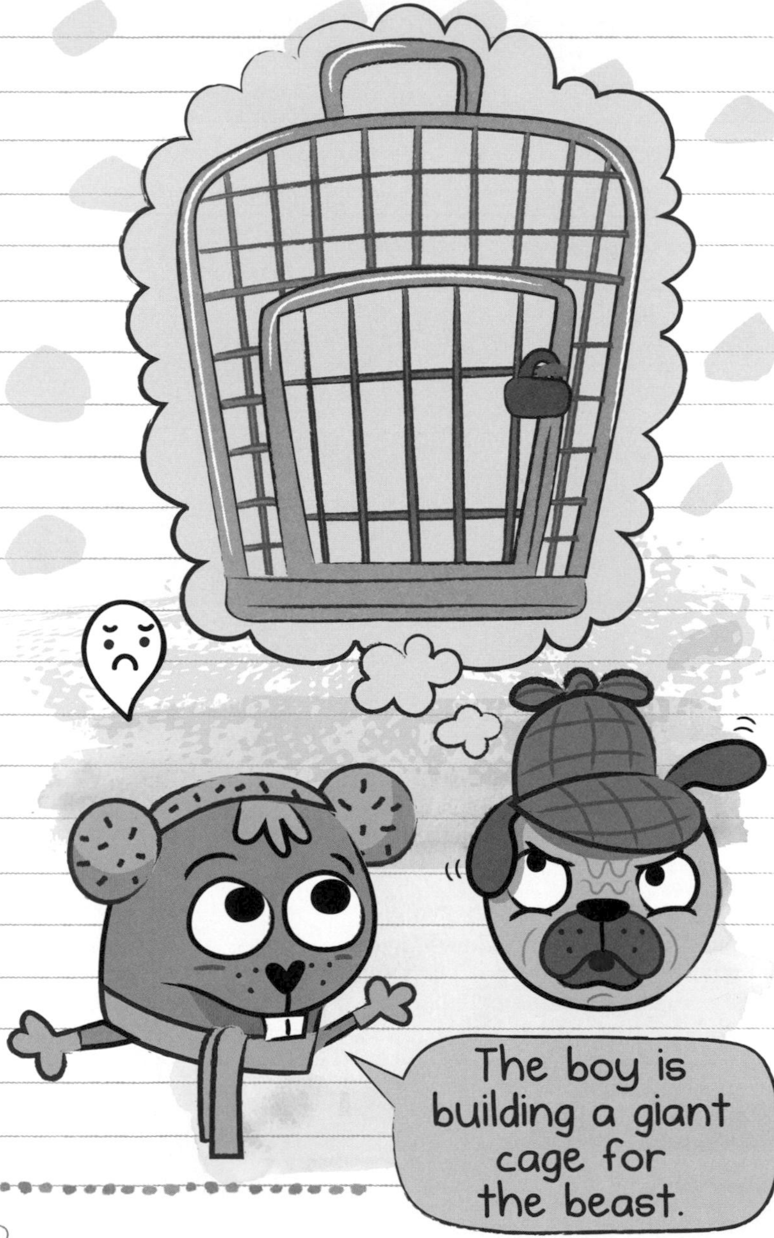
The boy is building a giant cage for the beast.

I wasn't sure I could trust Nutz.

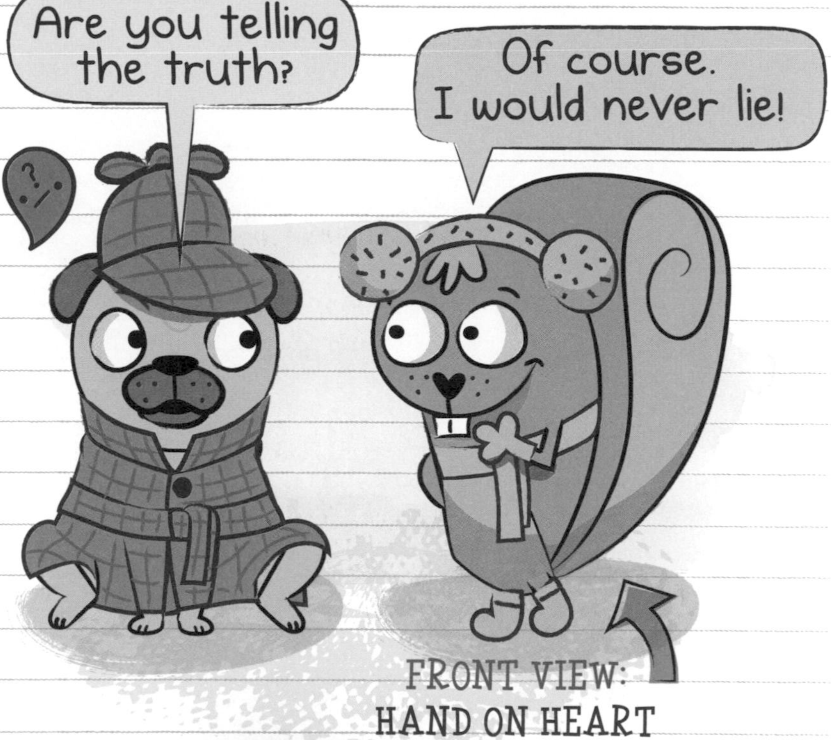
Are you telling the truth?
Of course. I would never lie!
?
FRONT VIEW: HAND ON HEART

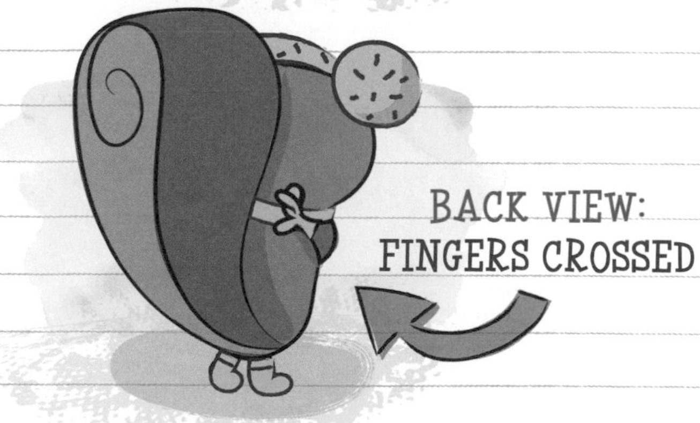
BACK VIEW: FINGERS CROSSED

Diary, remember when Nutz lied to me and told me peanut butter had been recalled? I threw away every jar I had. Later, I found out Nutz had eaten every last drop.

I knew I couldn't believe Nutz. I needed to see the monster for myself.

I made my way to the hole in the fence and peeked through.

I saw the monster's paws with my own eyes!

I rushed inside to safety. That night, I was too afraid to sleep.

Chapter 6

SNOW ESCAPE

FRIDAY

Dear Diary,

I can't spend another night like that. I didn't sleep a wink! All I could think about was that beast next door.

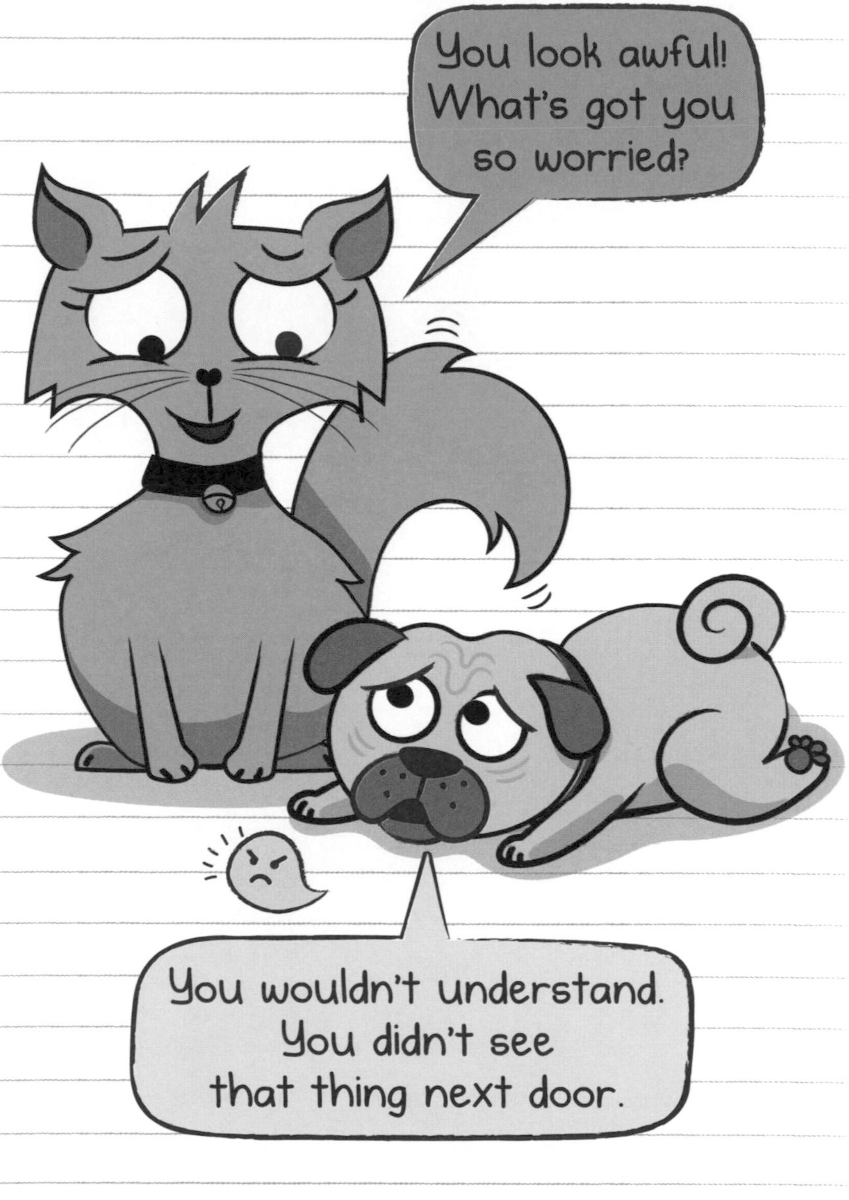
You look awful! What's got you so worried?
You wouldn't understand. You didn't see that thing next door.

I made my way outside to the snow fort. Nosy Nutz came over to pester me.

Nutz grabbed Bear and ran up a tree.

That's when it happened: Bear sailed right past me and over the fence!

I didn't want to go next door. But I couldn't leave Bear. Who knew what the monster would do to him!

Okay, I'll go. But you threw him over. You're on lookout.

I'll do it for some peanut butter.

It's always a deal with Nutz. But at least in the end he agreed to help for half a jar of peanut butter.

After digging a small hole, I squeezed under the fence. I couldn't believe what was on the other side. It was WAY worse than I had imagined.

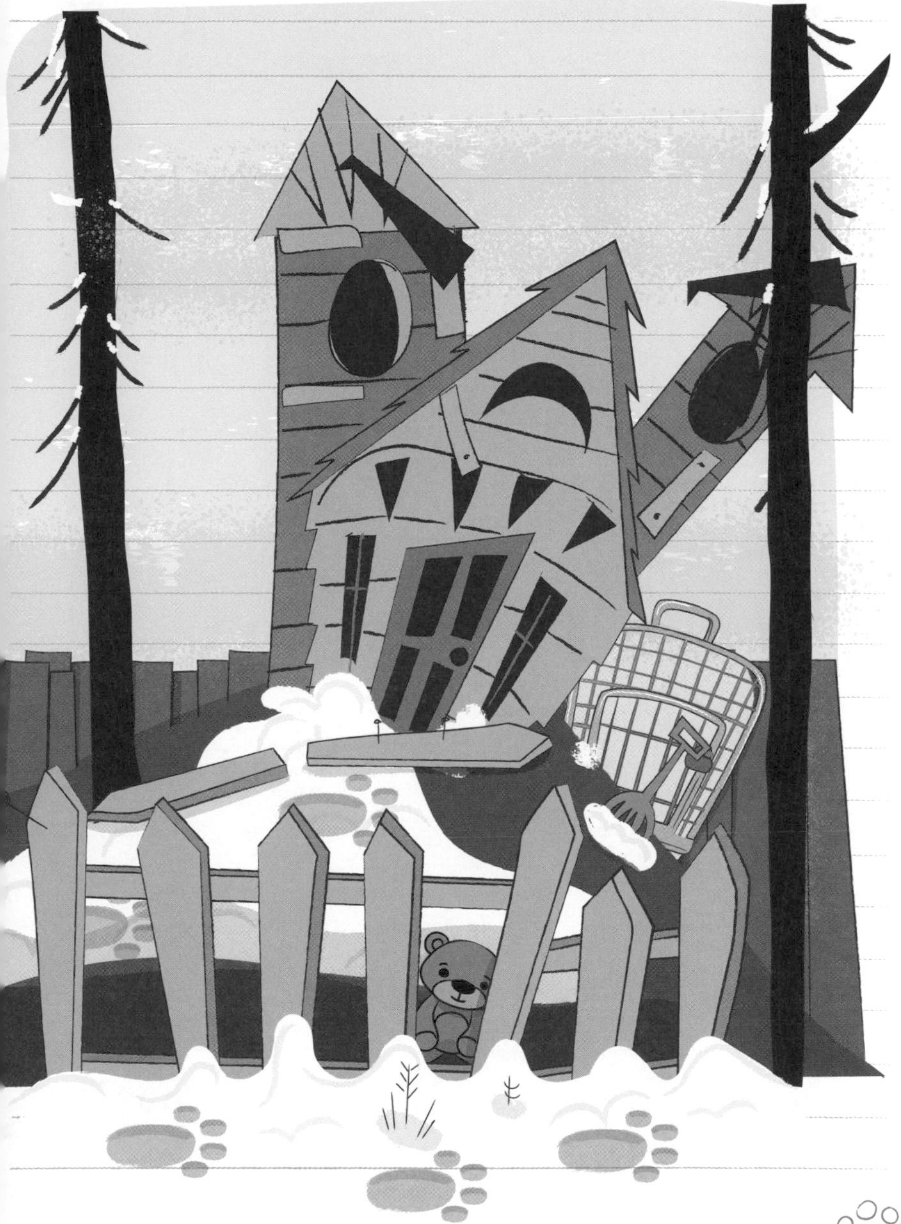

I thought the beast was big. But he's not just big, he's HUGE. His paw print was ten times bigger than mine!

And then I saw the cage Nutz told me about!

Even in the mess, it didn't take me long to sniff out Bear. I found him just in time.

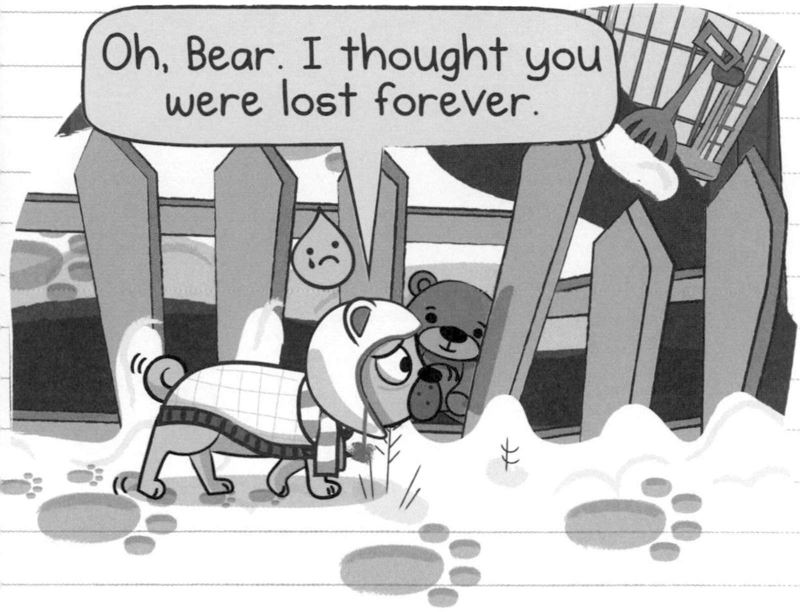
Oh, Bear. I thought you were lost forever.

But then Nutz sounded the alarm.

The monster was coming back!

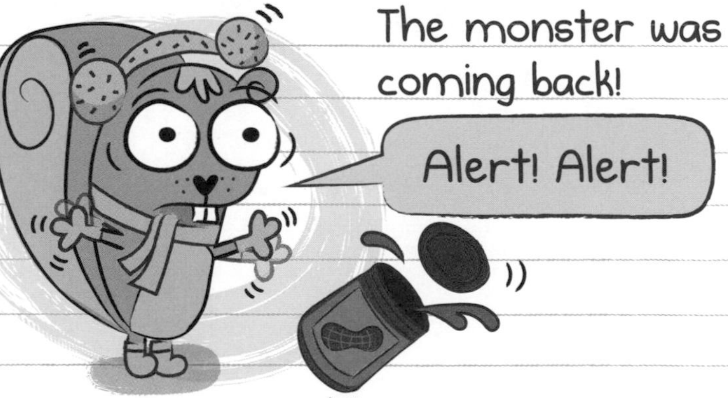
Alert! Alert!

Diary, it was such a close call. The beast almost got me! The playdate is only two days away, and I still haven't solved the mystery. What on earth IS that thing?!

Chapter 7

SNOW NICE TO MEET YOU

SATURDAY

Dear Diary,

Bella and I were both scared to go outside today. But Bella's mom said we had to get some fresh air.

Mom doesn't get how scary it is out here. I'm glad you're here with me.

Then something surprising happened.

An airplane came crashing down on our side of the fence! (It was a remote control toy airplane, but still!)

The plane was stuck in the side of our fort. Bella cleaned it off just as the boy next door climbed over our fence.

I'm so sorry!
I hope I didn't scare you.
I lost control of my airplane.
My dog's afraid of loud noises.
When she heard the airplane,
she crashed right into me!

It's okay.
I don't think it's broken.
I'm Bella and this is Bub.

I'm Jack.

Bella and Jack became friends right away. Turns out they had both been worried about Sunday.

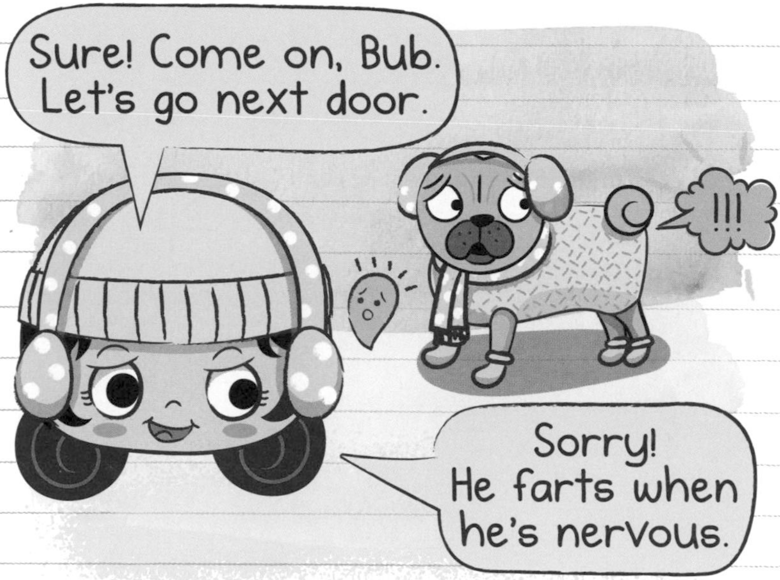
Sure! Come on, Bub. Let's go next door.
!!!
Sorry! He farts when he's nervous.

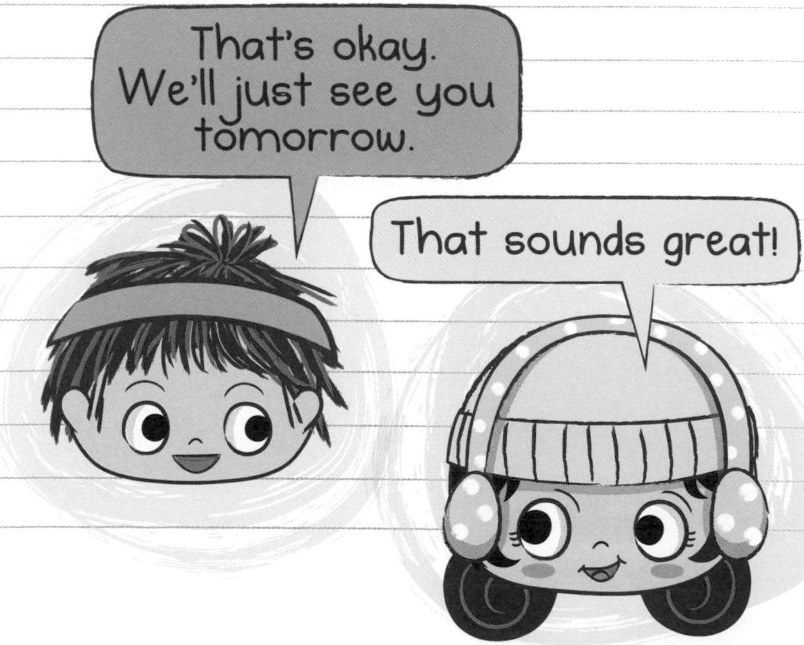
That's okay. We'll just see you tomorrow.
That sounds great!

Diary, I already knew what was next door: a beast!

We were so silly, Bubby. We let our imagination run wild! I like Jack. And I'm sure you'll like Luna, too.

I won't go! No! No! No!

Chapter 8

SNOW WAY OUT

SUNDAY

Dear Diary,

It was the day of the dreaded playdate. There was no way I was going. So I hid. But Bella found me and carried me outside. I couldn't escape!

> I can't wait to see Jack's backyard and meet his dog, Luna.

> This is going to be a disaster.

Jack's yard was cleaned up. But all I could see was how HUGE Luna was. Also, she was charging toward us at full speed!

Whoa! That's a really big dog!

Bub, meet Luna. I know she looks like a bear, but she wouldn't hurt a fly. Right, Luna?

What about a pug?

Diary, I was so glad Luna wasn't really a monster. But I could have done with fewer wet kisses.

Whoa, Luna! Easy does it. Nice to meet you, too.

Sorry! Sometimes I get carried away.

Okay, so I was wrong about Luna being a beast. I was also wrong about what Jack was building.

Wow! Is that a tree fort?

Yes, I've been working on it all week. Sorry about the noise and smoke. I had some problems with my tools. And I'm still not sure how I'm going to get my fort up there.

I bet we can help.

Bella and Jack built a pulley system. We all worked together to pull the fort up into the tree.

Bella and Jack built a ladder for them to use.

We couldn't figure out how Luna and I would get up there, though. But then Bella had a great idea.

We should add an elevator for the dogs! We can use the pulley system.

Yes! I have some old wooden boxes we can use, too.

The four of us fit perfectly in Jack's fort. Luna and I might just end up being good friends after all.

Diary, did you know snow forts don't last forever?!

I hope we get another snow day soon.

Me too!

Kyla May is an Australian illustrator, writer, and designer. In addition to books, Kyla creates animation. She lives by the beach in Victoria, Australia, with her three daughters and her daughter's pug called Bear.

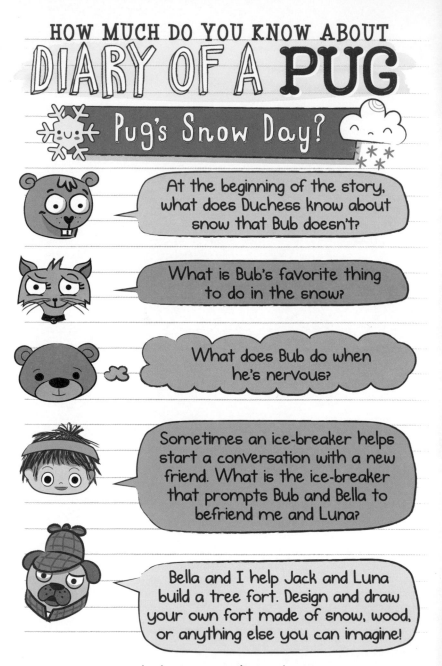

HOW MUCH DO YOU KNOW ABOUT
DIARY OF A PUG

Pug's Snow Day?

At the beginning of the story, what does Duchess know about snow that Bub doesn't?

What is Bub's favorite thing to do in the snow?

What does Bub do when he's nervous?

Sometimes an ice-breaker helps start a conversation with a new friend. What is the ice-breaker that prompts Bub and Bella to befriend me and Luna?

Bella and I help Jack and Luna build a tree fort. Design and draw your own fort made of snow, wood, or anything else you can imagine!

scholastic.com/branches